THE UGLY DUCKLING

HANS CHRISTIAN ANDERSEN
THE UGLY DUCKLING

as told by Marianna Mayer ⋀ illustrations by Thomas Locker

MACMILLAN PUBLISHING COMPANY

NEW YORK

COLLIER MACMILLAN PUBLISHERS

LONDON

Macmillan Publishing Company, 866 Third Avenue, New York, NY 10022
Collier Macmillan Canada, Inc.
First Edition
Printed in the United States of America

10 9 8 7 6 5 4 3 2 1

The text of this book is set in 14 pt. Meridien.
The illustrations are rendered in oil on panel,
made into color transparencies by
Gamma One Conversions, Inc.,
and reproduced in full color.
Library of Congress Cataloging-in-Publication Data
Andersen, H.C. (Hans Christian), 1805-1875.
The ugly duckling. Translation of: Grimme aelling.
Summary: An ugly duckling spends an unhappy
year ostracized by the other animals before he
grows into a beautiful swan.
[1. Fairy tales]   I. Mayer, Marianna.
II. Locker, Thomas, date, ill.   III. Title.
PZ8.A542Ug   1987   [E]   85-23869
ISBN 0-02-765130-4

For Maxie
— M.M.

For my father
— T.L.

It was springtime in the country. At the foot of an old castle encircled by a deep moat, a duck sat resting on her nest. She had been sitting like this for days and by now she was growing impatient for her eggs to hatch. The other ducks amused themselves by swimming in the moat and seldom stopped to visit. Indeed, she was beginning to feel quite sorry for herself when – finally – the eggs began to crack. Small, downy, yellow, duckling heads peeked out.

"Oh, welcome to the world, my darling ducklings," said the mother duck. "Look all around you at the wide, green world."

Of course they did, saying together, "How big it is."

"Yes," she agreed, and added, "bigger than you think, but you will soon see that for yourselves. Now, have you all hatched?" And she turned to check the nest. "Heavens, the largest egg is still not ready." She sighed. "We must wait, I'm afraid." And she settled herself back down upon her nest.

"How is your little brood?" asked an old duck who came by just then to pay her respects.

"One of my eggs, the largest of them all, is taking forever to hatch. But, as you can see, my other ducklings are doing quite well."

"And so they are," commented the old duck, who was fond of repeating the obvious. "Let me look at that egg," she went on. "I remember once finding a large egg in a nest of mine. It was a turkey egg, and how it managed to find its way into my nest I will never know!"

The mother duck raised her feathers to give her friend a better view.

"Oh, yes, I am sure it's a turkey egg. You will never get that creature to swim once it has hatched, mark my words. I say, leave it and take your others for a swim."

"Never mind," said the mother duck. "Since I've sat this long, I suppose I can sit a bit longer. I assure you I would know the difference between my own egg and that of a turkey. This egg is taking longer because it is so large, that's all."

"Suit yourself," said the old duck, and went on her way.

At last, the large egg cracked, and out tumbled a big and very peculiar-looking gray bird. The mother looked at him for one long silent moment, thinking, "He is certainly big for his age, and he doesn't resemble any of my other children. I wonder if he is a turkey after all. Well, we shall see."

The next day the sun shone bright in a beautiful blue and cloudless sky. The mother duck took her brood to the edge of the moat. "Everyone into the water," she ordered.

One by one, the ducklings dove in. They plunged their small heads right into the water and disappeared. Instantly, they popped up again and shook their heads with delight. They floated easily, knowing just exactly how to swim. Even the gray one did quite well for himself.

His mother was relieved. "He may be ugly, but he is certainly not a turkey," she told herself. "How perfectly he uses his legs, and how straight he holds his neck, even if it is very long. He is my own child indeed, and, though he's different, I think he's quite handsome."

Then, to her children she announced, "Come along now. I'm going to take you to the barnyard to introduce you to the neighborhood. But stay close to me and, for heaven's sake, look out for the cat."

As soon as they arrived, they heard a terrible row. Two groups of ducks were fighting over a fish head. In the confusion, the cat swooped into the middle of the fight and stole away the prize.

"You see, children, one can never be too careful, for the world is filled with surprises – some good, some bad," said the mother duck, wishing she were as swift and clever as the cat. "Now, hold your heads up. And, by all means, remember to bow to that duck over there, the one with the red scarf tied round her leg. She is a Peking duck and quite rare among our circle. She wears that scarf as a mark of great distinction, for she is a prize duck who will never be cooked for supper."

The other ducks gathered around the mother duck and her brood and quacked loudly.

"Well, look at the new family. I'm sure we ducks outnumber all the rest of the animals in the barnyard," one boasted.

"But look at that big ugly one. I'm glad he's not mine," said another.

"He's the ugly duckling!" shouted another with a loud laugh, and the others joined in.

Then a young duck from another family went to peck the one they called the ugly duckling, but, just in time, the mother duck flew to protect him. "You leave my child alone. You're only jealous because he will grow to be bigger and stronger than you are." But she was troubled, for she knew she would not always be there to defend him.

"Yes, he's big," shouted back the duck that had tried to bite him. "He doesn't look like the rest of us, and that's reason enough to hurt him. He doesn't belong."

"Savage!" replied the mother duck with dignity as she turned away with her children.

"Very handsome ducklings," remarked the Peking duck. "I'd keep an eye on that big one of yours. He may surprise you one day."

"Thank you, your ladyship," answered the mother duck. "He may not be handsome, but he has a good heart and swims remarkably well for his age, perhaps even better than my other children. He was in his egg too long. This is why he is so big. I think he will improve with age," she said, looking fondly down at him.

"I'm sure you are right, my dear," said the Peking duck. "Well, make yourself at home and, if you should find a fish head, you may come and share it with me."

And so the brood of new ducklings were made to feel at home in the barnyard.

But the poor duckling who seemed so ugly to the others was never allowed to feel at home. The hens, the ducks, and the fierce turkey cock with spurs upon his legs mocked him relentlessly. As though this was not bad enough, the woman who fed the animals kicked him in disgust when she tossed the grain.

Before long, even his brothers and sisters shunned him. Everywhere he went, he was shoved and pecked. The only peace he had was close to his mother's side. But she was an impatient creature and soon grew weary of defending him. "Go away," she told him. "Find someone to play with. You cannot cling to me forever."

No one wanted him. It was not hard for him to know. He did not complain, but the hurt welled up in his eyes and spoke of his pain. He told himself, "I cannot stay in the barnyard. I must run away." And, then, one day he did.

He rushed into the forest. As he flew over the tops of low bushes, he startled the wild birds nesting there, and they flew up and away from him.

"Even the birds in the wild think I'm ugly," thought the duckling. Blinking back a tear, he kept on running.

Finally, he came to rest in a great swamp just as the sun, red as blood, was going down. Here wild ducks made their home among the tall reeds. Too exhausted to go any farther, the duckling stayed the night.

The next morning, he awoke to the questions of a flock of mallards. "What kind of bird are you?" they asked.

The ugly duckling bowed low, hoping to appear polite, but he didn't know what to reply.

"You really are an ugly mallard, if you are one of us," they told him.

"But you can remain with us, if you wish," the leader of the flock said, "so long as you don't try to get above your station."

The poor duckling was not thinking of getting above anything. In fact, he couldn't imagine what that might mean.

He stayed with the mallards a few days, and then two wild geese came to the swamp. They were ganders, and they took a liking to the ugly duckling.

They told him, "You're an odd-looking sort, but if you would like to migrate with us, we'll be happy to take you along."

Suddenly, the terrible sound of gunshots rang out. The noise put terror into the hearts of all the animals in the swamp. Panic took hold of the ganders, and they flew straight up into the air.

"Bang! Bang!" Two more shots, and the ganders fell dead before the horrified duckling.

Again shots rang out, and a whole flock of wild geese flew up into the open. The swamp was filled with the sounds of hunters' guns, and gray smoke from the gunfire filled the air. The acrid smell burned the eyes and throat of the ugly duckling as he hid, too frightened to move, among the tall reeds. The hunters' dogs came splashing into the marsh. Wildly they crashed through the reeds, flushing out their prey.

The poor duckling didn't know where to hide. Then, all at once, a large dog stood staring down at him. The hound bared his teeth and snarled. Just as quickly, the dog turned away and dove into the marsh.

When he could catch his breath, the duckling thought, "Oh, for once I can be grateful for being so ugly. It has saved my life."

He stayed very still in the reeds, his head tucked tightly under his wing as the shots boomed through the swamp. Hours and hours passed and, finally, at sunset, there was silence. The duckling dared not stir till darkness fell. Then he ran. Out of the swamp he raced, across fields and meadows, never looking back.

He came to a wood, and there he found a lake where he could swim and dunk his head. In this quiet place he felt safe. He saw other ducks, but they paid him no mind; and again he was reminded of his ugliness.

Autumn came, and the days grew shorter. The leaves turned to burnished gold, then flame, and finally brown. From time to time a chill wind blew, carrying leaves through the air like flocks of helpless birds, only to scatter them upon the ground and lake. Now the clouds were gray and heavy all the time. The duckling rarely saw the sun anymore, and when he did it gave no warmth. It rained, but the showers were cold upon his back.

One evening at sunset, a flock of graceful white birds flew overhead. The duckling gazed in wonder at the sight. Something in him called out to them, and he yearned to join them but knew he could not. Their feathers were pure white, their necks long and elegant. The ugly duckling didn't know they were swans. He heard them call to each other, in flight, to keep close on their long journey to a warmer climate, where the lakes would not be frozen all winter long. He turned round and round in the water, never taking his eyes from them. Something made him screech out so sharply that he frightened himself.

The flock of swans disappeared. Tears came into his eyes, for he was certain he would never see the regal birds again. The sight of those creatures left him feeling worse than ever before. In despair, he dove down to the bottom of the lake and, when he surfaced, he looked up again at the empty sky. He felt forlorn and hopeless. "Will I never belong?" he wondered. Though he knew nothing about them, he loved the swans with all his heart.

The nights grew colder and colder. Winter set in with sleet and snow, the first the ugly duckling had ever seen. Watching the snow fall and cover the ground in silent white reminded him of the glistening white birds, and he longed for them all the more. He had to swim round and round to keep just a small part of the lake from freezing. But each night the space drew in on him and became smaller. On all sides the frozen lake creaked and groaned as it set like stone. Soon he did not have the strength to keep up his constant movement. The ice closed in, and his feet were locked in the frozen lake.

The next morning, a farmer saw him. He felt sorry for the helpless creature, so he walked out over the ice and broke the duckling free. The farmer carried the half-dead duckling under his warm coat, home to his wife and children, and the good woman brought the duckling back to life.

But when he revived he was very frightened. The farmer's children were excited and wanted to play with him. All he could think of was escape. He flapped his wings and accidentally fell upon their old dog, who barked in alarm. The duckling jumped out of the dog's way and right into a pail of milk. The children screamed with laughter and terrified the duckling all the more. They fell on top of each other in the scramble to catch him. But he was too fast for them. The front door was slightly ajar and he flew for the opening. Once out of the house, he hid in the snow-covered bracken. Try as they might, the family could not find him.

Somehow he managed to survive the hard winter, scavenging scraps in barnyards and seeking shelter in open barns, waiting for the first warm rays of the sun to return.

Spring at last did come. The sun shone bright again, and the mockingbird sang with piercing sweetness to his mate. The last traces of snow melted to reveal fresh meadow grass. The duckling sat among the reeds in the swamp and breathed the sweet scent of spring once more.

He spread his wings with joy and flew up into the sky. He felt strong, and his wings had grown quite large. He soared over the green meadow, past apple trees all in bud, and saw the lilac laden with blooms resting its boughs upon the lake.

Suddenly, out of the thicket came three swans. They fluffed their white feathers and glided gracefully into the lake. Immediately, the ugly duckling recognized the birds he loved so dearly. His heart leapt at the sight of them.

"I will fly over to them, just to get a better look, but I dare not disturb them," he told himself. "I know they will scorn me. Yet I must see them up close." Gently he alighted upon the water and swam cautiously toward the magnificent birds.

The moment they saw him, they arched their long necks and swam toward him. "As though," he thought with a start, "they are coming to greet me."

Humbly he cast down his eyes. He could already hear their harsh words, though they had not uttered a sound. At that moment he spied his own reflection in the water. Confused, he could not quite understand what he saw. There, mirrored in the water, was a splendid swan. He was no longer an overgrown, gangly, gray bird, but a swan. The three others were coming to meet one of their own. They made a circle around him and gently touched him with their beaks. He felt he would burst with happiness as he returned the gestures of friendship.

The farmer's children came down to the lake, carrying bread and cake to feed the snow white swans. They cast the food upon the water, and the swans swam to fetch it.

The girl smiled and said, "Look, there, isn't that the swan Father tried to save last winter?"

Her brother felt certain it was. They smiled to each other and said, "He is the handsomest of all."